Owen

Rheneas

Peter Sam

Luke

Skarloey

Paxton

Winston

The MOVIE Storybook

EGMONT
We bring stories to life

First published in Great Britain 2012 by Egmont UK Limited
239 Kensington High Street, London W8 6SA

Thomas the Tank Engine & Friends™
CREATED BY BRITT ALLCROFT

Based on The Railway Series by The Reverend W Awdry
© 2012 Gullane (Thomas) LLC. A HIT Entertainment company.

HiT entertainment

ISBN 978 1 4052 6444 0
52939/1
ingapore

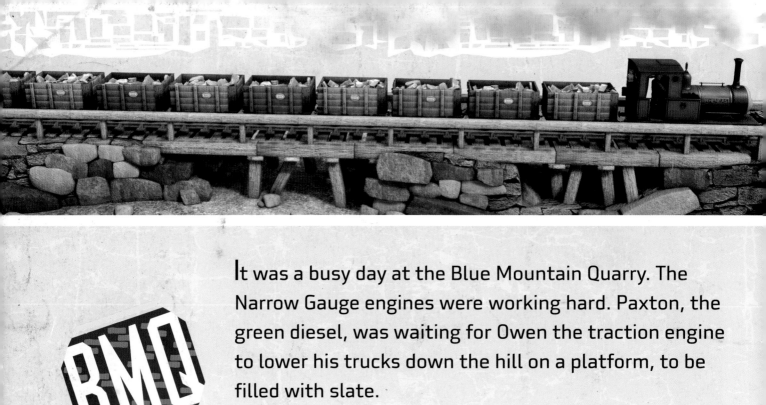

It was a busy day at the Blue Mountain Quarry. The Narrow Gauge engines were working hard. Paxton, the green diesel, was waiting for Owen the traction engine to lower his trucks down the hill on a platform, to be filled with slate.

Paxton coupled up to his trucks, but when he began to pull away, a huge brick came loose from Blondin Bridge, high above the quarry.

Then there was trouble! Rheneas was steaming towards the bridge, pulling his heavy slate trucks.

Rheneas tried to stop, but it was too late! His trucks pushed him onto the bridge. He pumped his pistons like never before and raced to the other side, just as the bridge gave way.

Rheneas hurtled away down the track, biffing and bashing the walls on his way. Finally he came to a stop.

"I'm all right!" he wheeshed, though he was badly scratched. "But I could do with a fresh coat of paint!"

Paxton was less lucky. Some bricks had fallen on top of him, knocking him off the track. He would need urgent repairs.

On Thomas' branch line, Thomas was having fun with his coaches, Annie and Clarabel.

Suddenly, they heard a strange sound. **HONK, HONK!**

"Cinders and ashes! What's that?" wondered Thomas, as a small, red car lurched around the bend, carrying The Fat Controller.

"This is Winston, my new track inspection car," announced The Fat Controller. "Thomas, I have a special job for you. Paxton has been in an accident at the Blue Mountain Quarry. I have arranged with The Thin Controller for you to work in his place."

Thomas whooshed down the track to the Blue Mountain Quarry. He loved to work with the Narrow Gauge engines.

Thomas worked hard all day, shunting slate with his friends. As evening fell, he chuffed to Brendam Docks to deliver his trucks. And that night, he slept soundly at Tidmouth Sheds, while his Narrow Gauge friends slept in the quarry hills.

The next morning, Thomas was shunting trucks in the quarry when he heard a rattle from inside a tunnel. A small green engine darted out, an engine Thomas had never seen before! "Hello, I'm Thomas!" the blue engine peeped cheerfully.

But the new engine didn't answer. He disappeared into another tunnel.

"How strange!" said Thomas. He puffed over to Sir Handel. "I've just seen a little green engine racing from one tunnel to another," said Thomas. "Who is he?"

"W ... well now," Sir Handel stammered, "it was probably a runaway truck, Thomas. There are lots of those up here." And Sir Handel steamed away.

Later, Thomas saw the little green engine dart out from behind a shed.

"Please stop!" Thomas called out. "Who are you?"

The engine didn't stop. Thomas couldn't follow him, as his wheels were too wide for the narrow gauge rails.

Thomas puffed over to a junction as Rusty rolled up. "Rusty, do you know a little green engine?"

Rusty turned red. "I think ... I'm sure I think ... it was a mountain goat," he babbled.

"It wasn't a mountain goat," Thomas said. "It was an engine!"

"I'm afraid I can't help then!" Rusty bustled, and he rolled away quickly.

"No one wants to talk to me!" huffed Thomas, and he puffed back down the track.

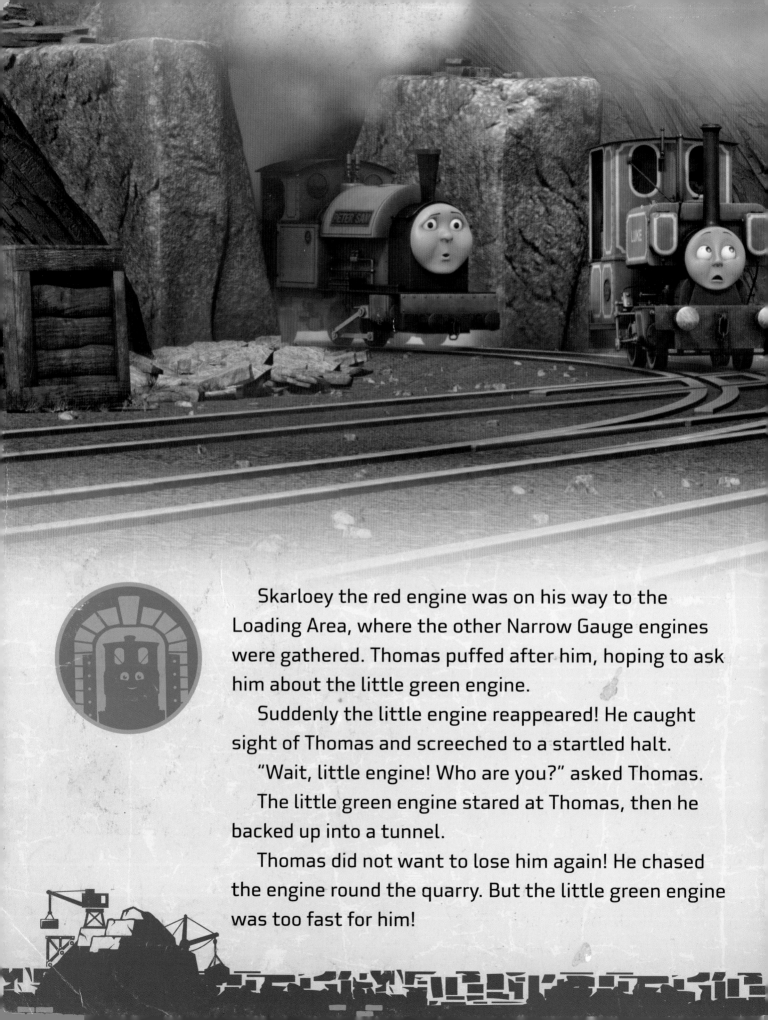

Skarloey the red engine was on his way to the Loading Area, where the other Narrow Gauge engines were gathered. Thomas puffed after him, hoping to ask him about the little green engine.

Suddenly the little engine reappeared! He caught sight of Thomas and screeched to a startled halt.

"Wait, little engine! Who are you?" asked Thomas.

The little green engine stared at Thomas, then he backed up into a tunnel.

Thomas did not want to lose him again! He chased the engine round the quarry. But the little green engine was too fast for him!

Rheneas puffed along the track and accidentally blocked the little engine's path, making him back into another tunnel and out of sight.

"I'm sorry, Luke!" Rheneas wheeshed. Thomas stared. So the engines did know who the little green engine was!

As Skarloey rolled up, Thomas asked, "Who is Luke? Why does he keep puffing away? Why will none of you talk to me about him?"

"Luke is a friend, Thomas," Skarloey said, gravely. "But you are our friend too. We trust you. What I am going to tell you, no one else must know. Once, long ago, Luke did something very bad. He thinks that if anyone finds him, he will be sent away from Sodor forever!"

That night, Thomas asked his friends at Tidmouth Sheds, "What do you all think is the worst thing an engine could do?" All the engines thought hard. Thomas reminded his friends of the time he had ignored a danger sign, and fallen into a mine!

"But it wasn't bad enough for me to be sent away from Sodor," sighed Thomas. *Was anything that bad?* he wondered.

The next morning, the Blue Mountain Quarry was busy. Rocky was moving the stones from Blondin Bridge. Thomas whooshed in, and sped over to Rheneas and Skarloey. Rheneas was complaining that he needed a new coat of paint as he was still badly scratched.

"I've asked my friends," Thomas peeped. "We're sure there is nothing an engine could do that is bad enough to be sent away from Sodor."

Skarloey looked sternly at Thomas. "Have you talked to the other engines about Luke?" he asked.

"No!" said Thomas. "I wouldn't do that. I'm trying to help Luke. I want to be his friend too."

"Very well, Thomas," said Skarloey. "Puff along now!"

Skarloey reversed down the track to continue his work. He didn't notice Rocky behind him, swinging a load of stones across the track.

"Rocky, watch out!" cried Thomas. "Skarloey, stop!" Skarloey braked just in time to miss Rocky's hook.

"Sorry, Skarloey! That was close!" panted Rocky.

"Fenders and fireboxes!" Skarloey steamed. "Thank you, Thomas. You saved me from losing my cab. You are a good friend."

Thomas smiled. He was pleased that Skarloey could trust him.

As Thomas worked, Luke puffed out of his tunnel
and rolled up beside him.

"Oh!" Thomas said in surprise. "Hello, Luke!"

"Hello, Thomas!" said Luke. "I'm sorry I hid from you.
I didn't know you, and I was scared. But now, well ...
I wonder ... would you be my friend?"

Thomas peeped proudly. "I'd like that very much,"
he said.

Thomas and his new friend worked very well
together. They were both Really Useful Engines.

Suddenly, the quarry echoed with the sound of a horn.
HONK, HONK!

It startled Luke, who darted out of sight again.

Winston whizzed around the bend, this time carrying both The Fat Controller and The Thin Controller. Winston screeched to a halt beside Thomas.

"I have news for you! Paxton is now fixed," said The Fat Controller.

"Thank you for all your hard work, Thomas," said The Thin Controller. "Paxton will now take over again."

With that, The Fat Controller pressed down on the throttle, and Winston roared away.

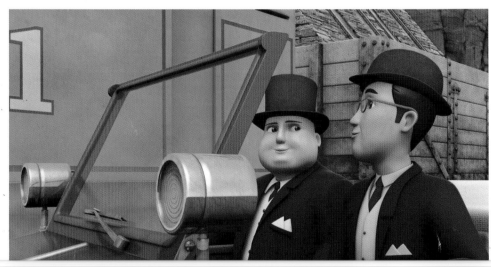

Thomas chuffed over to Luke's tunnel to say goodbye. "You don't have to hide from me," he said, gently. "We're friends now."

The little engine steamed slowly out.

"Why do you keep hiding, Luke?" asked Thomas. "Skarloey told me that you're scared you'll be sent away from Sodor. But I'm sure you won't be."

Luke looked worried. "But, Thomas, I did something very bad," he said.

"I've done bad things too," said Thomas, "and I'm still here!"

Luke laughed a little.

"I'll tell you what I did, Thomas," said Luke. "But no one else must know."

Luke took a breath, and told Thomas his story ...

A long time ago, I was sent to Sodor to work at the Blue Mountain Quarry. My boiler bubbled. It was my dream to work on Sodor!

There was a yellow engine on the boat. He came from far away. And he spoke a different language. A language I couldn't understand.

A storm was coming in. The sea was rough. But I was happy. I could see Sodor! I couldn't wait to be lifted onto the rails.

At Brendam Docks there was hustle and bustle. Cranes clanked. Dock Men shouted. The men wanted to lift the yellow engine off. But I wanted to be the first off the boat.

The Dock Men agreed. And I was happy. But then ...

"What, Luke?" said Thomas, bringing the little engine back from his memories.

There was a long, long pause.

"I knocked the yellow engine into the sea!" said Luke.

Thomas gasped, loudly. "But how?"

Luke said, in a hushed voice, "I bumped into him, and sent him splashing into the sea. The sound was terrible!"

I had to go to the Steamworks to be fixed. I heard the storm thunder outside. But I could only think about the yellow engine in the sea. He was there for a very long time. By the time they lifted him out he was rusty and ruined.

The yellow engine was never seen again. He must have been taken to the Smelter's Yard. He couldn't be Really Useful any more. And it was all my fault!

"That was a long time ago," said Thomas, softly.

Suddenly, Thomas and Luke heard Skarloey's voice: "Come along, Paxton! What are you standing there for? Get those wheels whirring!"

Paxton bolted out from behind a row of trucks.

"What are you doing here?" asked Thomas in alarm.

"I've ... um, I've come to take slate to the Docks," Paxton stuttered. "That's my job again. Excuse me!" And off he sped down the tracks.

Thomas looked back towards Luke. But the little green engine had gone.

"Goodbye, Luke," Thomas called into the tunnel. "I have to go back to my branch line now. But I will come back. Remember, I am your friend."

The next day, Thomas asked Toby to work on his branch line, while he set out to find the yellow engine.

At the Dieselworks, Thomas discovered plenty of engine parts, but none of them were yellow.

But as Thomas rolled out onto the forecourt, he heard something that made his boiler run cold.

Paxton was telling Diesel all about Luke! "... and that's when Luke knocked the yellow engine into the sea," said Paxton. "The yellow engine was *never* seen again!"

"We don't want an engine like that on our Island!" said Diesel. "He could knock any of us into the sea! We'll tell The Fat Controller, who'll tell The Thin Controller. Together they'll send Luke away *forever!*"

Thomas did not want to hear another word. He thundered off down the track. Paxton and Diesel saw Thomas leave. "We must hurry to the quarry, Paxton!" said Diesel. "Thomas is a tricky tank engine. Whatever he's doing, we must find out!"

As Thomas whooshed down the track, an idea flew into his funnel. Luke had said the yellow engine had been rusty when it was pulled out of the sea ... *Where else would you take a rusty engine?* thought Thomas. *The Steamworks of course!*

Thomas puffed to the Steamworks. "Victor, do you remember fixing a yellow engine that fell into the sea? He spoke a different language."

Victor stopped pulling freight. "*¡Calderas hirvientes!*" he gasped.

"What did you say?" asked Thomas.

Then he realised Victor was speaking a different language!

"Cinders and ashes!" Thomas declared. "It was you, Victor! You were the engine that fell into the sea! Please tell me what really happened."

So Victor took a deep breath, and told Thomas his story. It matched Luke's story, up until the part when the storm gathered over the ship.

"With one big wave," said Victor, "the chains holding my wheels broke! I was no longer held to the deck. I was in danger! I called to the crew for help, but they didn't understand me, so they didn't help me."

A crane lifted the little green engine first. He swayed on the end of the hook ... and bumped into me. I could do nothing. There were no chains to stop me! I slid into the sea! **SPLASH!**

Because the weather was so bad I was left in the sea for a long, long time. And when I was finally lifted out, I was in a terrible mess.

"You must have been very frightened," said Thomas.

"Yes, it was scary," said Victor. "But the scariest thing of all was that no one understood me. So I learned your language. My first word was 'red'!"

"Why red?" asked Thomas.

Victor gave a smile. "Because, my friend, I had to be repainted. And red was the colour I chose. A bright, new colour for my new life on Sodor!"

Thomas raced from the Steamworks. He had to reach the quarry before Diesel and Paxton. He had to tell Luke the truth!

Luke puffed out from the quarry hills to greet Thomas. "Luke, I have wonderful news!" wheeshed Thomas from the quarry floor. "I talked to Victor! He told me what really happened when you were being unloaded from the ship! He said ..."

Skarloey interrupted him. "We told you not to talk to the other engines!" he scolded.

All the engines were cross, even Luke. "We thought you were our friend, Thomas," they said together, "but you're not!"

Diesel's horn echoed around the quarry. The engines stopped and stared as he oiled up by Thomas, with Paxton close behind him. Diesel looked up, and saw Luke at the top of a hill.

"Are you the engine that pushes other engines into the sea?" Diesel scorned. "I've heard all about you!"

The engines moved away from Thomas. "Don't listen to Diesel!" Thomas cried. "Let me explain!"

But Thomas knew that his friends thought he had let them down. He felt terrible.

Thomas puffed to the foot of the hill and begged
Rocky to lift him onto Owen's platform so he could
reach Luke and talk to him.

Owen started to pull Thomas slowly up the hill.
All the time, Diesel shouted up at Luke, "Thomas can't
help you. What you did was bad! You'll have to leave
the Island!"

Luke believed what
Diesel said. He backed up
as Thomas rose towards
him. "Don't listen to him,
Luke," Thomas shouted. "I
know what happened. You
didn't do anything wrong!"

When Thomas reached the top of the incline, he shot off the platform to chase after Luke.

Then there was trouble! Thomas had forgotten that his wheels were too wide for the narrow gauge rails.

Thomas tried to back up, but his wheels wouldn't grip. He slipped and slid forward until he was hanging over the edge of the cliff. Thomas was in great danger!

Luke buffered up to Thomas, who looked very worried. But the little engine smiled kindly. "I'll pull you back. I can do this. I'm your friend," said Luke.

He coupled up to Thomas, and pulled with all his might. "Hold on, Thomas!" he said, and he heaved Thomas back from the edge of the cliff.

Thomas laughed in relief – but he wasn't out of danger yet! Luke helped him onto Owen's platform, but Luke slipped and slid onto the platform too. It groaned under the weight of the two engines, gave way and hurtled towards the quarry floor!

Owen tugged at the winch in panic to slow down the platform, and it finally bounced to a stop on a lower level of the quarry.

All the engines whistled and cheered, glad that the two friends were safe! Nobody noticed that Paxton had disappeared ...

Suddenly, the engines heard **HONK, HONK!** as Winston rattled into the quarry, carrying The Fat Controller and The Thin Controller.

The Fat Controller was very cross. "Thomas, whatever are you doing? You're supposed to be back on your branch line, not here in the quarry!" he boomed. He ordered Rocky to bring Thomas and Luke down.

Devious Diesel slid forward. "I can explain, Sir," he said. "That little green engine there is called Luke. He's a bad engine. He knocked a yellow engine into the sea! Thomas has been hiding him here."

Thomas had no time to explain to The Fat Controller, as Paxton shunted Victor into the quarry on a flatbed.

"I have come to meet an engine I have not seen for a long time. His name is Luke," said Victor. "You didn't push me, Luke, I slipped off the boat. It was an accident!"

"It can't be you," Luke said, staring at Victor. "You're not yellow. And you don't speak a different language."

Victor laughed. "*Buenos dias*, Luke. *Me llamo* Victor," he said. Luke gasped. "I *was* yellow," said Victor, "but I was painted red when The Fat Controller had me repaired!"

For the first time in a long time, Luke was happy. He was grateful to Thomas for finding out the truth. "Thomas is my hero," he told The Fat Controller. "And he's my friend."

A few days later, Thomas went to the Steamworks. Luke was there, with Victor.

"Hello, Thomas!" Victor said. "I know you were looking for a yellow engine. Well, I think I've found him!"

Rheneas rolled out of the Steamworks smiling widely. He had been given a brand-new, bright yellow coat of paint! Thomas beamed from buffer to buffer. A bright new colour really did mean a new life for his friends.